Ginger the Stray Kitten

Also by Holly Webb:
Max the Missing Puppy
Buttons the Runaway Puppy
The Frightened Kitten
Little Puppy Lost

Ginger the Stray Kitten

by Holly Webb

Illustrated by Sophy Williams

tiger tales

For Sophie

tiger tales

5 River Road, Suite 128, Wilton, CT 06897
Published in the United States 2015
Originally published in Great Britain 2009
by Little Tiger Press
Text copyright © 2009 Holly Webb
Illustrations copyright © 2009 Sophy Williams
ISBN-13: 978-1-58925-183-0
ISBN-10: 1-58925-183-0
STP/1800/0066/0215

10 9 8 7 6 5 4 3 2 1

For more insight and activities, visit us at www.tigertalesbooks.com

Chapter One

"Are we going past the farm today?" Rosie asked her grandma hopefully. They had a few different ways back from school to Grandma's house, but the road past the farm was Rosie's favorite. Grandma wasn't usually in a rush, and she didn't mind walking slowly while Rosie stopped to look at any cats she happened to meet on the way. Rosie loved cats and was desperate for one of her own, but she hadn't managed to persuade her mom yet.

Grandma smiled at her. "Oh, I suppose we could go that way. I need to pick up some eggs from Mrs. Bowen. I might make a cake tonight, as it's the weekend." She looked down at Rosie and said thoughtfully, "But you know how she likes to chat, Rosie. Are you sure you won't get bored?"

Rosie looked up at her in surprise, and realized that Grandma was teasing. Grandma knew that Rosie loved going to the farm, because Rosie could go and watch the stray cats in the barnyard. There were lots of them, and Grandma said they were called feral cats because they weren't anyone's pets. Rosie had never managed to count them all, but she thought there were probably about 20 of them. Mrs. Bowen put food out occasionally, but mostly they lived on the mice they caught in the barn.

Rosie loved to imagine that the cats belonged to her, but they weren't really very friendly. If she sat on the foot step of the old rusty tractor for a while, they might prowl past her, but none of them would come to be petted.

One of the prettiest cats, a tabby with beautiful spotted markings, had given birth to a litter of kittens about five weeks before. Rosie had heard them meowing in the barn, but she hadn't been able to see them for a while, as the tabby cat had hidden them under some old hay bales that were stored in there.

Now the kittens were all running around the barnyard, and they weren't quite as shy as the older cats. Rosie was hoping that she could tame one of them. She couldn't help dreaming of taking a kitten home for her own pet.

She knew which one she wanted – the gorgeous little orange girl kitten. The kitten was so sweet – she had orangey-creamy fur with darker orange stripes, and a bright pink nose. Her eyes were green and very big, and Rosie thought she was the prettiest cat she'd ever seen.

Sometimes people called Rosie Ginger because of her long, curly red hair. Mom had always told her that her red hair was pretty and different, and that she'd like it when she was older, but Rosie wasn't so sure. Then she had seen the kitten. Rosie felt like she and the kitten were a pair, with their beautiful coloring. They were proud of it!

She wished the kitten would let Rosie pet her. Rosie could just imagine how soft her fur would be. The other day the kitten had come close enough to sniff at Rosie's fingers, but she'd darted off again without letting Rosie touch her.

Grandma called hello at Mrs. Bowen's door, and Rosie looked eagerly around the barnyard. She had something special for the cats today, and she was really hoping she could tempt the tabby kitten to come over to her. Rosie had noticed at lunch that her friend Maya had ham. Mom usually gave Rosie peanut butter and jelly, because that was her favorite, but she couldn't help thinking that the kitten would love Maya's sandwiches. Maya had been picking at the ham with a bored expression.

"Don't you like your sandwiches?" Rosie had asked, a plan starting to form in her mind.

"I wanted peanut butter, but my brother ate it all," Maya had sighed. "I hate ham…."

"Do you want to trade? I only have one left, but it's peanut butter and jelly," Rosie had offered hopefully.

"You sure?" Maya had looked delighted. "I didn't know you liked ham. You can have both of them!"

Rosie had slowly eaten one of the sandwiches, and then tucked the other one away in her lunch box.

Maya had watched her put it away.

"Didn't you like it?" Maya asked.

Rosie had leaned over closer to her. The kitten felt like a special secret, and she didn't want everyone to know. "I'm saving it. Remember the pretty tabby kitten I was telling you about that lives on the farm near my grandma's house? She came right up to me the other day, and I bet if I had some food she might even let me pet her. You don't mind, do you?"

Maya had shaken her head. "Of course not! Oh, you're so lucky, going to see kittens. Are they tiny?"

"The lady who owns the farm thinks they're about five weeks old. They're so cute! Maybe your mom would let you come home with us and see them

12

one day. I'm sure Grandma wouldn't mind."

Now at the farm, Rosie unwrapped Maya's sandwich, and started to crumble it into little bits, very gently, trying to keep as still and quiet as she could. It didn't take long for the cats to get a whiff of the delicious, meaty smell.

Rosie caught a movement out of the corner of her eye, just a streak of black fur. It was one of the kittens, peeking its head around the tractor wheel. Suddenly, several more little cat faces popped up, their whiskers twitching as they sniffed the air.

Rosie threw a bit of sandwich on the ground, and the closest kitten, the black one, pounced and swallowed it whole. Then he looked up for more. All the other kittens padded a few steps forward, not wanting to miss out. This time Rosie dropped the food closer, and one of the tabby kittens darted in and grabbed it, running back to a safe distance before she dared to stop and eat.

Rosie's heart thumped with delight as she saw her favorite orange kitten patter across the yard, eager to join in. Rosie tried to throw the next piece close to her, but the tabby kitten got there first and gobbled it up. The orange kitten gave Rosie a pitiful stare. *I'm so hungry*, the kitten seemed to be saying. *Pllleeeease feed me....*

This time Rosie threw her an extra-large piece. The orange kitten held it down with one paw, and hissed protectively when the others circled around her. Rosie laughed – the kitten's face was so funny – and the others looked up at Rosie, their eyes wide. Then they all ran back to their hiding places.

"Oh, no!" Rosie muttered, wishing she hadn't been so noisy.

But the orange kitten had only run a couple of steps away from her piece of sandwich, and now she eyed it uncertainly. Food – but also the noisy girl. What should she do? She eyed Rosie. She'd seen the girl before. The girl didn't usually make any noise, and she was quiet now. She wasn't even moving. And she still had lots more of that sandwich.

The kitten darted over and gulped down her piece, then looked around. Her brother and sisters were still hiding. If she went closer, while they weren't here, she might get *more* sandwich…. Nervously, ready to run just in case, the kitten edged closer, her eyes on the ham.

Rosie carefully tossed her a little bit, much closer to Rosie's feet this time.

The kitten stared at her suspiciously. Rosie looked back. Maybe it was too close. But then the kitten moved one paw forward, then the other, and then she was just close enough. The kitten started to gobble the sandwich, one eye on Rosie.

When it was gone the kitten sat up, licking her whiskers. She cast a quick look behind her. The others were all watching, but they weren't coming any closer. The food was all hers! She knew it was risky, but the sandwich was too delicious. She had to have more!

Rosie couldn't help smiling. The kitten was only about three feet from Rosie, almost close enough to touch. Instead of throwing the sandwich, Rosie held out her hand with the last pieces in it.

The orange kitten stared at Rosie nervously. What was she supposed to do now? The smell of that sandwich was so good. She could run up and grab it. So she skittered forward, her whiskers trembling, and quickly licked up a few crumbs from Rosie's hand, before stepping back to watch her again.

Then the kitten heard a noise and looked around. Her brother and sisters were starting to creep closer! They'd seen that she wasn't afraid, so they were getting braver, too. If she didn't wolf that sandwich down fast, she might have to share it.

The orange kitten hurried back to Rosie and started to eat as fast as she could, licking the crumbs away with her rough little tongue. Rosie had to try hard not to giggle – the kitten was tickling her!

Soon, the kitten had eaten it all. She glared at Rosie's hand, obviously wondering when it was going to produce some more.

"Sorry, it's all gone," Rosie whispered. "But I'll bring you some more next time. I bet Mom would let me have ham sandwiches if I asked, and I'll give them all to you."

The kitten eyed her expectantly, and Rosie stretched out her hand. The kitten licked it, but there was no more ham.

Rosie gently petted the top of the kitten's head, and the kitten jumped in surprise, looking up with huge emerald eyes. *What was that for?* she seemed to be saying. Rosie guessed she wasn't used to being petted. It made Rosie feel sad.

"Rosie! Where are you?" It was Grandma, calling from the farmhouse door. The orange kitten raced for the safety of the barn at top speed, chasing after her brother and sisters, and Rosie sighed as she got up. Still, she had managed to pet the orange kitten! She was so little and thin, but her fur had been so soft, exactly as she'd imagined. More than ever, Rosie wanted a kitten just like her....

Chapter Two

Rosie thought about the orange kitten all weekend. It was such a big step that the kitten had let Rosie pet her! Maybe she really would be able to tame the kitten. She was young, after all.

Rosie sat at the kitchen table, drawing pictures of the kitten while Mom made a shopping list. It was so hard to get the stripes right, and she had to keep starting again.

"That's beautiful, Rosie!" Mom said, leaning over.

Rosie shook her head. "Her face is more of a peachy color. I don't have the right pen for it."

"Is it a real cat?" Mom asked. "One of the ones you see on the way home from school?"

"She's a kitten at Mrs. Bowen's farm," Rosie explained. "You know, the little farm down the road from Grandma's house? There are five of them altogether. You'd love them, Mom."

Rosie looked hopefully at her mother. Maybe if Mom came and saw how cute the kittens were, she'd let them take the little orange one home. If only Rosie could tame her....

"She does look cute," her mom agreed. "Just be careful, though. Those wild cats probably have all kinds of horrible illnesses."

Rosie sighed. That didn't sound very hopeful....

Rosie's mom couldn't understand why Rosie was so excited to get to school on Monday morning.

"What's gotten into you, Rosie? Usually it's me telling you to get a move on, not the other way around."

Rosie just smiled. The sooner she was at school, the sooner it would be time to go home, and she could persuade Grandma to take her to the farm again. She just couldn't wait to get there.

She'd made sure Mom bought ham for her sandwiches this week, and she'd begged for an extra yogurt so she could save both sandwiches and not have her tummy rumbling all afternoon.

Luckily, Grandma didn't mind going to the farm again. Rosie ran ahead as they went down the road that led past the farm, calling to her grandma to hurry.

"I can't walk any faster, Rosie," said Grandma. "You really do love those cats, don't you?" She frowned a little as she said it, but Rosie was thinking about whether the orange kitten would remember her and didn't notice.

It seemed to Rosie that the cats appeared more quickly this time when she sat down on the old tractor. They remembered her as the food person. The orange kitten was the first to appear, her wide, white whiskers twitching with anticipation. Rosie wished the kitten wasn't so nervous, and that she could bring her home and take care of her. Rosie crumbled the sandwich and scattered a few pieces around, hoping the kitten would be brave enough to come close.

The orange kitten sniffed the air. More ham! The others weren't as brave, so she could have most of it to herself. She was sure the girl wasn't dangerous – she *had* touched her last time, but very gently. It had been quite nice. She'd even let the girl pet her again, if there was ham.

Rosie watched hopefully as the orange kitten crept forward, and she held out a particularly yummy-looking piece of ham. The kitten nibbled it delicately, then bumped Rosie's hand with her forehead, as if to say thank you. Rosie held out her left hand with more sandwich, and carefully rubbed behind the kitten's ears with the other.

The kitten looked up at her, still confused about why the girl wanted to pet her like this, but not minding too much. She even purred a little. Her ears were itchy, and the girl was rubbing the right spot.

The orange kitten finished the last of the sandwich and stared at Rosie, sniffing her fingers to see if more food would appear. When it didn't, the kitten yawned, showing her pink tongue, and jumped on her sister's tail, starting a kitten wrestling match.

Rosie watched them, giggling quietly to herself. They were so funny! Maybe tomorrow she would bring a piece of string for them to chase. She was sure they would like that.

The kittens suddenly scattered, and Rosie turned to see her grandma coming out of the farmhouse and waving good-bye to Mrs. Bowen. Grandma looked worried, and Rosie jumped up.

"What's the matter?" Rosie asked, as they headed toward the road.

Grandma looked at her and sighed. "I've been meaning to talk to you about this for a while, Rosie," she said. "Mrs. Bowen is moving – she's going to live with her son in town. The farmhouse is a bit too big for her now that she's on her own."

Rosie stared up at Grandma in surprise. She couldn't imagine the farm without Mrs. Bowen. "Oh. So who's going to live at the farm now?" she asked. "Is Mrs. Bowen selling it?" There was no For Sale sign up.

"No...," Grandma said. "Well, yes, I guess she is. The land has been sold to a developer – they're going to knock down the farm buildings and put up some houses instead. Mrs. Bowen signed the contract with them a little while ago, and she's been gradually packing her things up and moving them over to her son's house. She's leaving the farm this week."

Rosie gasped. It was all happening so quickly. Then a horrible thought struck her. "But Grandma, what's going to happen to the cats? They won't stay around when the farm's a building site! Where will they go?"

"It's all right, Rosie," Grandma said, putting an arm around her shoulders. "Mrs. Bowen has asked the people from the rescue shelter to find homes for the cats. They're going to come and get them tomorrow, she told me.

It'll be much better for the cats, you know. They'll check them out, and find good homes for the kittens. As for the older cats, they'll try and find someone with farm buildings or stables who'll keep them as outdoor cats, like they are here."

Rosie nodded. "But I won't see them anymore," she said sadly, her voice quivering. "Not even the little orange kitten, and she was starting to like me, Grandma, she really was. I … I even thought of trying to take her home, if I could persuade Mom…."

"I'm not surprised she liked you, considering you were feeding her your sandwiches." Grandma smiled at her. "Mrs. Bowen does have windows, Rosie!"

"Oh." Rosie looked at Grandma, her cheeks a little pink. "You won't tell Mom, will you?" she asked.

"Well, no. But I think you'd have been better off eating the sandwiches yourself and buying some cat treats with your money," Grandma suggested.

"I don't think your mother would like to know she was making sandwiches for a tribe of wild cats."

"It won't matter now anyway," Rosie said tearfully. "I'll never see any of them again!"

When Mom picked Rosie up from Grandma's that night, she was surprised by the quiet, sad little figure who came down the stairs.

"What's up, Rosie? Did you have a bad day at school?" she asked.

Rosie shook her head.

"Go and get your things, Rosie," Grandma said, and by the time Rosie had packed up her homework and her pencil case, Grandma had obviously told Mom what was going on, because she didn't ask again.

Rosie stared miserably out the car window as they drove back to their house. The rescue shelter people would be thinking about new homes for the kittens already, she supposed. Rosie wondered who would get to adopt the orange kitten. Maybe it would be a girl her age. But no matter who it was, Rosie was sure no one would ever love the kitten as much as she did. She was so jealous.

Suddenly, Rosie sat up straight, staring out of the front window in excitement. Why shouldn't that girl be her? The kitten needed a new home, and she already liked Rosie. She could name the kitten Ginger!

Now Rosie would have to persuade her mom, of course.

"What is it, Rosie?" her mom asked. "A rabbit didn't run in front of the car, did it? I didn't feel anything."

"What? No! Mom, can we have a kitten?" Rosie begged. "Please? All of Mrs. Bowen's cats need homes. Please can we?"

Mom didn't say anything for a minute, and Rosie stared at her hopefully. At least she hadn't said no right away.

"I don't know, Rosie," Mom said. "It would be nice to have a pet – but those kittens are wild. They aren't used to people. I don't know if we'd be the right home. Someone who knows more about cats would be better, I think."

"We could learn about cats!" Rosie pointed out eagerly. "And those kittens really, really need homes, Mom. The rescue shelter people are coming to get the cats tomorrow. They'll hate being in cages. There's one of the kittens, Mom, who's really sweet, and she's already almost tame. She lets me pet her and she even eats out of my hand. She'd be a wonderful pet!"

"Well, I'll think about it. Maybe we could go and see how tame they really are. I'm not sure I want a wild kitten climbing my curtains...."

Rosie beamed. She was sure that Ginger was hers already. The kitten was so cute that Mom just wouldn't be able to resist her!

Back at the farm, the orange kitten curled up next to her mother and brother and sisters in a pile of hay in the old barn. It made a cozy nest, and she licked her paw sleepily. She was thinking about that girl, and wondering if she would come back tomorrow. She might bring more food, and maybe she would pet her fur again. It was nice when she did, like her mother licking her ears.

The kitten snuggled closer to her tabby sisters and closed her eyes. The hay was soft and warm, and she quickly fell asleep, never dreaming that everything was about to change.

Chapter Three

The next morning, the kittens were startled awake by a vehicle driving into the yard. Mrs. Bowen didn't have a car, and she took most of her eggs to town to sell, so very few people drove up to the farm. The kittens blinked at each other, then peered blearily over the edge of their nest. The kittens' mother, the spotted tabby cat, went to stick her nose around the old barn door. The orange kitten followed, eager to see what was going on. She wriggled between her mother's front paws, staring out into the yard.

Mrs. Bowen was standing by the back of a van, next to two girls. One of the girls opened up the doors and started to unload some boxes. The van smelled strange, the kitten thought. She'd never smelled anything quite like it before. And what were those wire box things?

Her mother was tense beside her, her whiskers pricked out as she watched what was going on. The kitten's brother and sisters were starting to meow, as they smelled the fear scents on their mother and the other older cats who were watching, too. They just didn't trust humans. The tabby cat backed into the barn so that her orange baby wasn't between her paws anymore, and butted the kitten hard with her nose.

The orange kitten looked around in surprise. What was wrong? Was this a game? Then she saw that her mother's eyes were wide with fear, and the fur had risen all along her back. This was no game. The mother swiped the kitten with her paw, sending her into the yard, and then she hissed at her with her ears laid flat. It was quite clear what she was telling her kitten to do.

Run!

The orange kitten scooted quickly out the barn door, heading for the old tractor. The tire had come away from the wheel, and the orange kitten had found this wonderful hiding place while she was playing. There she waited, her heart thudding with fear, trying to figure out what was going on.

Her mother had darted back into the barn to try and fetch her brother and sisters, and some of the other cats were trying to make a run for it, too. But as soon as they'd seen that the cats knew they were there, the two girls had quickly put a net around the barn door. Now they'd put on gloves, and they were catching the cats with strange things around the neck.

Ginger watched in horror as one by one her brother and sisters were caught and placed into wire cages. She could hear them meowing frantically as the cages were loaded into the van. Then one of the girls walked right up to the tractor where she was hiding.

The kitten edged back as far as she could go, trembling. She didn't want the girl to see her, but now *she* couldn't see what was happening. Where were they taking her brother and sisters? Were they all in that horrible-smelling van? Had they caught her mother, too? Her tail thrashed from side to side as the girl walked past, searching – for her, maybe. Ginger curled herself into a ball, her eyes wide with fear.

"I just caught the last one. I'm glad I had my gloves. She was struggling like anything!" shouted a voice from across the barnyard. Ginger then listened as the girl walked away from the tractor and the van doors slammed shut.

As the van drove off, a small bright-pink nose peeked out from the wheel of the tractor. Ginger watched the van rattling out of the farm gate, carrying her brother and sisters away from her, and gave a miserable little meow. Should she try to follow them? But she was sure her mother hadn't been happy about where they were going. Where was her mother? Maybe she would come and get her now that the people were gone. Or should she try to find her mother?

Ginger crept out of her hiding place and searched the yard. There was no sign of any other cats at all. But she couldn't believe that her mother had left her. She wouldn't! Even if they had caught her, she would have gotten away somehow.

Ginger wandered around the outside of the barn, meowing sadly, and wishing her mother would come back soon, because she was hungry. Maybe she'd gone hunting for a mouse for breakfast. Yes, that was it.

As the morning wore on, Ginger got hungrier. She searched around for her mother and meowed pitifully for her, but still she didn't come.

At last she went a little closer to the farmhouse, drawn by the smell from the garbage cans. Mrs. Bowen had cleaned out her fridge and cupboards, and there were some black plastic bags lying there. The kitten pawed at one of them hopefully and clawed a little hole, grabbing some old cheese.

She nibbled at it. It wasn't great, but it was better than nothing.

She ate all of it, her whiskers twitching at the strange taste. She wished the girl would come back and feed her more of that delicious ham. She had been surprised when the girl had petted her, but she'd liked it. If the girl came back now, Ginger wouldn't be on her own. If only *somebody* would come!

Rosie practically dragged Grandma to the farm after school.

"All right, Rosie, all right! But we can't stay long. Mrs. Bowen is still packing. She's moving tomorrow. She won't want us bothering her today," Grandma said firmly.

"I know, but I need to find out about the kittens, whether the people came today. Mom said we could stop by the rescue shelter on the way home!" Rosie looked up at her grandma with shining eyes. "If she likes Ginger, we could even take her home this afternoon!"

Grandma smiled. It was great to see Rosie so excited, although she wasn't sure Rosie's mom would agree to a kitten right away.

Mrs. Bowen waved to them from the kitchen window. She was piling china carefully into a big box, and looked a bit hot and tired.

"Did they come?" Rosie asked her excitedly. "Did they take all the kittens to the rescue shelter?"

Mrs. Bowen smiled. "Oh, yes, dear. This morning."

"Do you have the address?" Rosie asked hopefully. "Mom says we can look at the kittens – she might even let me keep one of them! The sweet little orange one, you know?"

Mrs. Bowen wrote it down, and Rosie folded the piece of paper and tucked it carefully in her pocket.

Mom had said she'd try to leave work early so they could go to the rescue shelter that evening, and now Rosie sat by Grandma's front window, watching for her car. When her mom arrived at last, she dashed out to meet her.

"The kittens are at the shelter! I've got the address, Mom. Come on, they're only open until six!" she cried.

Her mom laughed. "All right! But remember, we're just looking. I know you want to take that kitten home, but I still need to think about this. Anyway, I can't imagine we'll be allowed to take one of them yet. They'll need to be checked by a vet to make sure they're healthy."

Rosie nodded. "But at least let's go and see!" she pleaded.

Secretly, she was sure that as soon as her mom saw Ginger, she would give in. Maybe they wouldn't be able to take her home today, but they could still tell the rescue shelter people that they wanted her!

The rescue shelter was in the next town. The girl at the reception desk knew about the kittens, and she smiled at Rosie's eager questions.

"I'm sure you can go and see them," she said. "We wouldn't usually let people visit the kittens until we'd checked them out, but since you already know them…." She led Rosie and her mom to a room at the back, with large cages in it.

Rosie spotted the tabby mother cat at once. She was prowling up and down the cage, looking anxious.

"Oh, she really doesn't like being shut in. And she must be upset that she's not with her kittens," Rosie said sadly.

The girl from the rescue shelter nodded. "I know. But because she's a feral cat, we need to separate her kittens from her now. It's so the kittens can get used to humans and give them the best chance of settling in at their new homes. They're in that cage at the end. Want to see them?"

"Oh, yes. Come and see, Mom!" Rosie whispered, grabbing her mom's hand and pulling her along.

"Oh, they are sweet!" her mom agreed, peering through the wire. "Look at that little black one!"

But Rosie was staring anxiously into the cage. There were four kittens in the basket, curled up asleep – one black, and three tabbies. There was no pretty little orange kitten.

Ginger wasn't there!

Chapter Four

"Don't cry, Rosie," Mom said as they walked back to the car.

Rosie was trying not to cry, but there were just a few tears that she couldn't seem to stop. She was thinking about what could've happened at the farm when the cats were caught.

Why hadn't Ginger been with them? Probably she'd found a way out of the barn and slipped away. But why? Maybe she'd been scared of the rescue shelter people, but it was also possible that Ginger had stayed behind to wait for her. Maybe Ginger hadn't wanted to go because of Rosie, because Rosie had been feeding her and playing with her.

Rosie had read about feral cats on the internet and knew that they were good hunters, but Ginger was too young to hunt for herself. Her mother would still have been catching food for her kittens. Without her mother to feed her, she might starve. Rosie nodded firmly. She had to go back to the farm. She just had to find Ginger, no matter how long it took.

Rosie was determined to look for the kitten the next day, but she and Grandma were shocked when they reached the farm. Grandma had come another way to get Rosie from school, and they both stopped in surprise as they came close.

"My goodness, that went up so quickly!" Grandma exclaimed.

A huge wire fence was now surrounding the barnyard, covered in big notices about wearing hard hats, and no children playing on the building site. It was a building site already!

Rosie pressed her face up against the wire fence. The barnyard was deserted, with no sign of life at all.

"Can't we go in and look for her?" she asked Grandma.

"No, Rosie. Look – it says no one can go in. We'll just have to keep coming by and hope we see her – or maybe we could ask the builders to keep an eye out. There's no one here now, but I'm sure there will be soon; otherwise they wouldn't have bothered to put the fence up, would they?"

Grandma was right. The next day, a couple of men in yellow hard hats were wandering around the building site with a little machine that beeped. It took Grandma and Rosie forever to catch the men's attention, but at last one of them came over.

"Yes?" he asked.

"Have you seen a kitten?" Rosie said nervously. "There were some cats here, and they were taken to a rescue shelter, but we think one of the kittens ran away...." She trailed off. "We just wondered if you'd seen her? An orange kitten?"

"No, sorry." The builder turned away. Rosie didn't dare call him back, even though she wanted to.

"Could you keep an eye out for her, please!" Grandma called, and Rosie squeezed her hand gratefully. She'd wanted to ask that, too.

They continued walking, Rosie looking back sadly every so often. They seemed to be able to see that fence no matter how far away they were.

"Don't give up hope, Rosie," Grandma told her. "You never know."

But Rosie couldn't help feeling that her chances of finding Ginger were getting smaller and smaller. What if she had escaped before the fence went up? Maybe Ginger wasn't there at all!

Ginger was hiding between two hay bales in the barn, peering out occasionally, and trembling as the men's heavy boots thumped past the door. Who were they? And why were they stamping and crashing around her home? She wished her mother and her brother and sisters would come back, but she was sure now that they were gone forever. If her mother had still been here, she would have come to find her by now, wouldn't she?

Ginger had hidden in the barn when the men put the fence up, and she'd dashed back there again this morning. She didn't dare do more than poke her nose out a bit occasionally to see if they were gone. She was starving, and it was getting harder to find anything to eat in the garbage bags by the farmhouse.

There were voices outside now. Were more people coming? She wanted the farm to go back to being quiet and safe like it was before. Ginger listened miserably, but then her ears pricked up. She knew that voice. It was the girl! She was there! Maybe she'd known Ginger was hungry and had brought her some more sandwiches! Ginger edged nervously around the barn door, the fur on her back ruffling up.

The men were still there, and the girl was talking to one of them. If only they would go, Ginger could run over to the girl. Ginger meowed a tiny meow, hoping the girl would hear. The kitten didn't dare call loudly in case the men saw her.

No! The girl was leaving!

Rosie walked sadly down the road with Grandma, leaving the kitten staring desperately after her.

The girl was gone, and Ginger didn't know if she would come back. Ginger felt so small and scared, and very, very alone....

Chapter Five

On Friday, Grandma was waiting outside school for Rosie as usual. It was raining, and Rosie was taking a while. She and Maya were among the last few to come out, and Maya had her arm around her friend.

"Rosie's really upset about Ginger," she explained to Rosie's grandma.

"I just don't think I'm ever going to

see her again," Rosie whispered sadly.

"You can't give up!" Maya said firmly.

Maya's mom had come up and was giving Rosie a concerned look. "Is everything okay, Maya?" she asked, and Maya explained about Ginger being missing.

"Poor little thing," her mom muttered. "Have you tried putting food out to tempt her, just in case she's still around?"

Rosie lifted her head. "No, we haven't. We should try that! Can we do that today, Grandma? Oh, I should have saved my sandwiches for her!"

"You could buy some cat treats at the pet store!" Maya suggested.

"Sammy loves those, especially the salmon-flavored ones."

"Please!" Rosie begged. "I'll pay you back, Grandma."

Grandma smiled. "I think we can get some cat treats. Come on."

"I wish I could come with you, but I have dance class," Maya said. "I'd love to see Ginger. I bet she'll come out for those cat treats."

"Thanks for the great idea," Rosie told her gratefully, and she and Grandma set off for the pet store.

"Call me and let me know if you see her!" Maya yelled after them, and Rosie turned back to wave. Maya had understood why she was so upset. She adored her fluffy white cat, Sammy. He'd been lost for a couple of days last year, and it had been awful.

Rosie chose the salmon treats, like Maya had suggested. Sammy was handsome and liked his food. Ginger was sure to like them, too.

They walked quickly over to the farm. Down the road, they could hear banging and the rumbling sounds of big vehicles. Rosie and Grandma exchanged a look and sped up to see what was going on.

The farm looked so different. The builders were knocking down the barn! A huge yellow digger was thundering past them on the other side of the fence – even Rosie felt scared by how big and loud it was. How would a kitten feel!

"Oh, no!" Rosie cried. "That's where the cats all used to sleep!" She watched as the digger tore at the walls. She clung to the fence, pressing her face against it so hard the wires marked her forehead, and looked frantically around the site. She couldn't see the kitten.

"Ginger isn't there, is she?" she asked, her voice shaking. "You don't think she was in the barn, when they started pulling it down…."

Grandma stared through the fence at the builders and their machines. "I don't know, Rosie. Ginger could be hidden because she's frightened. She might want to come out, but she doesn't dare." Grandma put her arm around Rosie.

"Try the cat treats," Grandma suggested gently. "Why don't you scatter a few through the fence? Maybe the smell will tempt her." She helped Rosie tear open the packet. "My goodness, I would think she could smell that from miles away. They're very fishy, aren't they?"

The treats did smell very strong, and Rosie pushed a few through the mesh of the fence. Then they waited, watching the builders in their bright yellow vests and hard hats as they cleared away the broken pieces of wood that were all that was left of the kitten's home. But there was no sign of Ginger – no long, white whiskers peeking out from behind a hay bale, no orange tail flicking around the corner of the farmhouse. The kitten was nowhere to be seen. After 10 minutes, Grandma turned to Rosie.

"It's starting to rain harder, Rosie. We'd better go, but we'll try again. Maybe your mom will bring you over tomorrow or on Sunday. We won't give up."

Rosie nodded, feeling slightly better. She would never give up on Ginger.

Even though she was only across the yard, Ginger hadn't seen the girl. The kitten was hiding under the abandoned tractor, shuddering each time the digger crashed through her old home. Ginger had run out as soon as the builders had come into the barn. She was wet, cold, and hungry, and now she didn't have anywhere to sleep!

Since the barn was destroyed, Ginger made a decision. This wasn't her home anymore. She realized now that her mother wasn't coming back. She needed to find somewhere new to live.

Maybe she could go and find that nice girl with the sandwiches?

Rosie's mom took her back to the farm on Sunday, and they stood by the fence calling for a long time.

"Put some more cat treats down," Mom suggested. "Then at least Ginger will have something to eat."

Suddenly, Rosie gasped. "Mom, look!"

"What is it? Did you see her? I can't see anything." Mom peered through the fence.

"No, that's it! I can't see anything. That's the point! The cat treats I put through the fence on Friday are gone!"

"Are you sure?" Mom asked.

"Definitely. I was right here, so they should be just on the other side of the fence. Ginger's been here. She's eaten them! Oh, Mom!" Rosie beamed at her, feeling so relieved. She bent down to empty some more cat treats out of the packet.

"Rosie, what's that?" Rosie looked up to see her mom pointing across the yard, down to the side of the farmhouse. "Can you see? It looks like something orange, by the garbage…."

Rosie jumped to her feet. Mom was right. Slipping along the side of the farmhouse was a flash of orange fur. It had to be Ginger!

But then the creature slunk out further into the yard, sniffing at the piles of wood from the barn. It was a fox, with a bright-white tail tip.

"Oh no...," Rosie breathed. It wasn't very big, but compared to a tiny kitten it was huge. "It might hurt Ginger, and oh, Mom, I bet it was the fox who ate the cat treats!"

Mom sighed and nodded. "I'm afraid it could have been, yes."

Sadly, they turned and walked away, Rosie blinking back tears. She had promised herself she wouldn't give up, but it was starting to look hopeless....

That evening, Rosie's mom was determined to cheer Rosie up. A television show they both liked was just about to start, and Mom hurried upstairs to get her.

"Rosie!" she called, opening her bedroom door. "Are you coming downstairs? Oh, Rosie!"

Rosie was sitting huddled on the floor, leaning against her bed.

"What's the matter?" Mom asked, sitting down on the floor beside her. "You're crying!"

"I'll never see Ginger again." Rosie sniffed. "What if she's hurt?" she whispered. "She might have been injured when the barn was knocked down. Maybe she got trapped. Maybe that fox ate her!" Tears rolled down Rosie's cheeks again.

"Ssshh, Rosie, don't say that." Mom hugged her close. "I don't think foxes normally attack cats. You're imagining the worst; the kitten might be fine. She's probably just staying hidden because she's afraid." She stroked Rosie's red hair. "You love this kitten, don't you? You've tried so hard to make friends with her – Grandma told me how patient you were, trying to get her to like you."

Rosie's mom hesitated. "Rosie, we could try adopting one of the other kittens at the rescue shelter…. What about the little black one?"

Rosie looked up, her eyes horrified and still teary. "We can't! We can't, Mom!"

"I mean, if we don't find Ginger," her mom explained gently.

Rosie shook her head. "Ginger's special," she said. "She's unique, too, like me. But it isn't just that. She seems so bright, and she's got so much bounce…."

She twisted one of her red curls around her finger, deep in thought. Ginger *was* special. And if she couldn't have Ginger, she didn't want another kitten.

Chapter Six

Ginger had felt brave when she decided to leave the farm and look for a new home. She had waited until all the people were long gone, and the farm was quiet. She would find somewhere comfortable. Maybe she'd find that friendly girl with the food.

But she hadn't realized that the

fence went all around the farm. It was very high, and it was struck down tight to the ground. Ginger couldn't get out! Scratching at it didn't work, and when she tried climbing it, she fell. At last she had slunk away to find a place to sleep. She'd hidden herself in Mrs. Bowen's woodpile, near the farmhouse. It wasn't comfortable, but it felt safe, far away from the builders' noisy, smelly machines.

The mice seemed to have been scared away by the men, too. Ginger had almost caught one, but the mouse had slipped into a hole, leaving Ginger hungrier than ever. It had seemed so easy when her mother did it. Ginger found some fishy-tasting round things by the fence over the last couple of days, but they hadn't filled her up. She'd seen a fox hanging around, and she had a feeling it had picked all the best pieces out of the garbage bags, because there was nothing left.

Now Ginger could feel herself growing weaker. Even though the rain leaked through into her woodpile nest and soaked her, she'd been grateful for it, as at least she wasn't thirsty. She'd been able to lap the water caught in the old buckets that were lying around the yard. But she needed food. She'd smelled delicious smells like the sandwiches the girl used to bring. They had been very good. She hoped the girl might come back, but probably she didn't like the big machines either, Ginger thought, as she drifted into a restless sleep.

Ginger was awakened by the smell of ham sandwiches. A builder had stopped for lunch and was sitting on one of the big logs. The smell was irresistible. Ginger uncurled herself and crept out. The sandwiches were in an open box next to the man. There was one left, and out of it trailed a piece of wonderful ham. She had to have it. Ginger looked up at the man. He was staring across the yard. He wouldn't notice, would he?

Ginger thrust a paw into the box, hooking the bread with her claws.

"Hey! Get out of there, you!" The man swiped at her with his hand! Ginger shot away, without even a morsel of bread to show for it. She raced up the tree that had been left standing in a corner of the yard by the fence, and crouched flat on one of the branches, quivering with terror. She looked down fearfully, digging her claws into the bark. She had never climbed a tree before, but instinct had taken her to the safest place. The man hadn't followed her.

Ginger stayed there for hours, too scared to move. By the middle of the afternoon, she felt it was safe to come down from the tree. It wasn't as easy as going up. She hadn't really *thought* about going up; she'd just done it.

She looked down from her branch – the ground seemed so far away.... She was stuck!

Rosie only got through school that day because Maya kept nudging her, reminding her that Mrs. Wilkinson was watching. Rosie would manage to listen or concentrate on what she was supposed to be doing for about five minutes before she started thinking about Ginger again.

Maya was coming to Grandma's today, and they were planning to look for Ginger together. Rosie was glad – Maya was so enthusiastic about looking for Ginger. Rosie had been disappointed so much that it was hard to keep her hopes up.

Maya jogged ahead as they came up to the farm. "Wow! It really is a building site. Oh, Rosie, poor Ginger. She must be really scared with all those people around, and those great big diggers. It's so noisy!"

Rosie nodded sadly and looked wearily through the fence into the yard. It looked so different now, with the barn gone and the yard covered in piles of rubble. Rosie wasn't expecting to see anything. But what was that in the tree over there? Rosie peered through the fence and grabbed Maya's sleeve.

"Maya! Grandma! Is that a cat in the tree? On that branch, there. No, no, there, look!"

A flash of orange fur showed among the leaves. It was hard to see if it was a cat, but *something* was moving.

"You could be right...," Maya said doubtfully. "I can't quite see."

Grandma was squinting through the fence. "I can't tell, either...."

"I am right! I know I am!" Rosie looked at them eagerly. "She's there, she really is. Yes, I can see her stripes! Oh, I can't believe it, I'd almost given up. Ginger! Ginger! I don't think she can hear me, with all this noise." She frowned. "Oh, Grandma, she must be so scared with all this going on. We have to get her out, we just have to!"

Rosie dashed along the fence, with Maya racing after her, and shouted to one of the men walking by. "Hey! Excuse me! Over here, please listen!"

But the man just walked past, pushing a wheelbarrow. He didn't even look at Rosie and Maya. Rosie rattled the gate, but no one seemed to hear her.

Grandma came up, looking anxious. "Rosie, calm down!"

"I can't make anyone listen!" Rosie looked at her wildly. "They have to let us in so we can go and get Ginger!"

Grandma pulled them gently away from the gate. "Girls, come back. It's a building site. I don't think they'll let us go in. Look, that man's coming out. We'll ask him." Grandma smiled politely at the man, who gave them a curious look.

"Excuse me, but have you seen a kitten around at all? She used to live on the farm, and she's disappeared. We think we might have just seen her in that tree."

The builder shook his head. He didn't look very interested. "No cats, sorry," he said, starting to shut the gate.

"She *is* there!" Rosie cried. "We've just seen her, we know she's there. You've knocked down her home, and you might have hurt her! You have to let us find her!"

The builder looked confused, and Grandma hugged Rosie tight. "Look, I'm sorry. The girls are very worried about the kitten. We really do think we saw her a minute ago. Could you please just keep an eye out for her?" She pulled an old receipt out of her bag and scribbled on it. "This is my phone number. If you could call us if you see her, we'd be so grateful."

The man took the note and stuffed it into the pocket of his reflective vest. Then he locked the gate, and walked off. Rosie watched him go, tears running down her nose. She was pretty sure he'd never look at the note again.

Grandma guided Rosie and Maya away from the gate. She was worried the builders might get annoyed and tell them to stop hanging around.

From in the tree, Ginger had heard the voices. It was the girl! The one with the food, who had petted her. The girl had come back for her. Ginger was sure that was why the girl was there. She tried desperately to get down the tree trunk.

But now the girl was going! Ginger meowed frantically, *please wait!* But no one heard her. Ginger took a flying leap from halfway down the tree trunk, and raced over to the fence.

Come back! Come back! I'm here!

But it was too late.

Chapter Seven

When they got back to Grandma's house, Grandma made Maya and Rosie sit down and have a drink.

"You can't get so worked up, Rosie!" Grandma said. "You can't help that kitten if you're shouting at people and getting into trouble, can you?"

Rosie sighed. Grandma was right. "I just don't think he was even listening,

Grandma," she said sadly. "That's why I was so angry. That man just said no cats, without even thinking about it!"

"But you saw her, Rosie!" Maya put in. "Ginger is still there! That's really good news! That was your orange kitten, wasn't it?"

Rosie smiled at last. "I'm sure, really sure. It was her pretty striped fur. I could see it through the leaves. She was up in that tree, I know she was. I wish she'd heard me, but it was just so noisy. I bet she would have come down, to see if I had sandwiches again." Rosie frowned. "I hope she wasn't stuck. That tree's enormous."

"Well, all we can do is go again tomorrow. As long as we're back in time for your mom to pick you up, I don't mind how long we stay. If we're there when the builders are gone, it'll be easier." Grandma smiled. "If she's there, we'll find her."

"Couldn't we go back now?" Rosie pleaded. "I'm not sure I can wait until tomorrow…."

Grandma shook her head. "It's getting late now, and you both still need to have a snack. We can go right after school tomorrow."

"Okay," Rosie sighed.

Ginger sat by the fence and howled. The girl had been here, and she'd missed her! Ginger scratched desperately at the fence, hoping to chase after the girl, but it didn't budge. She was still trapped.

Ginger trailed sadly back to the woodpile, avoiding the builders. At least the girl had come back. Maybe she'd come again tomorrow?

Rosie raced along the road, hardly hearing Grandma calling to her to slow down. She was desperate to get to the farm and see if Ginger was still there. At last she reached the fence by the tree. She wound her fingers through the wire, gazing hopefully up at the tree. There was no glint of orange fur. Rosie sighed. Still, she couldn't expect Ginger to be in exactly the same place she was yesterday.

Ginger is there, she told herself firmly. *You just need to look.*

Rosie tiptoed along the fence, trying to peer through. The awful thing was, Ginger might be asleep somewhere, just out of sight! She could miss her so easily.

Suddenly, Rosie gasped. It was as though all her breath had disappeared. Ginger was there! The kitten was crouched under the wheel of the old tractor, where Rosie used to tempt her with ham sandwiches. Ginger's ears were back, and she was watching the builders. Rosie's heart thudded as she saw how thin Ginger was.

Rosie crouched down by the fence. "Ginger!" she whispered, not wanting to scare the kitten, but of course Ginger didn't hear her. Rosie tried again, a little louder, and Ginger's ears twitched.

"Ginger!" Rosie waved to her as well this time, and she saw Ginger's eyes widen. The kitten had seen her! She stood up slowly, cautiously, and crept across the yard toward Rosie, moving one paw at a time and glancing around fearfully.

Rosie's eyes filled with tears as she saw how scared Ginger was. "Hey, Ginger!" she whispered, as the kitten stopped in front of the fence.

Ginger stood hesitantly, staring at Rosie, and gave a very small meow. Had the girl come back for her?

"Oh, Ginger, I'm so glad to see you!" Rosie said. "Are you all right? You look okay, just really thin." She giggled. "I don't know why I'm asking you questions. It isn't as if you can answer...." Very slowly, Rosie reached into her bag. "Look, I've got your favorite." She opened up her lunch box, pulling out the sandwiches she'd saved. "Yummy ham, Ginger, come and see!"

Ginger ran toward her. The girl *had* come back! And she'd brought food. Ginger was still nervous, but the girl had always been gentle, and the food smelled too good to resist. Although Ginger was half-wild, she'd been used to Rosie feeding her from when she was tiny. Ginger sat on the other side of the fence and meowed hopefully.

"Here you go, it's okay," Rosie said, pushing pieces of sandwich through the fence. Ginger gobbled them down eagerly. "You look like you haven't eaten in a week," Rosie told her. Her eyes widened. "Actually, it *is* a week, isn't it? You must be starved. Here, have some more."

"Rosie, I can't believe you've already found her! I won't come closer in case I frighten her off, okay? I'll just stay back here." Grandma leaned against the fence on the other side of the road, watching Rosie and the kitten.

Ginger finished the sandwich and sniffed, looking for crumbs. The sandwich had helped, but she still felt hungry. She wondered if the girl had any more. Ginger looked at her uncertainly, and edged forward. The kitten was sniffing at Rosie's fingers. She even licked them, in case the girl tasted like ham, but she didn't.

Rosie giggled – her tongue was tickly – then scratched Ginger's ears. Rosie could only just reach – the holes in the fence were too small for her whole hand to go through. "How are we going to get you out?" Rosie muttered, as she stroked Ginger's head with one finger.

Ginger ducked her head shyly, rubbing herself against the wire. It was warm, she ate, and now someone she liked was fussing over her. She closed her eyes and started to purr, very quietly, her tiny chest buzzing.

Rosie could feel Ginger trembling with the purr as she leaned against the wire. Rosie almost felt like purring herself, and a huge smile spread over her face.

"She's purring!" Rosie whispered to Grandma. Rosie was just starting to wonder if she should call to a nearby builder, and ask him to pick Ginger up and bring the kitten out to her. They wouldn't want a kitten getting in their way....

Then the man tripped and dropped the bucket he was carrying. It hit the ground with a loud clang. Ginger leaped into the air in fright, and Rosie jumped, her heart thumping.

Ginger had disappeared, streaking across the yard in a panic, and Rosie looked anxiously around for her, clinging sadly to the wire fence. Ginger had trusted her – the kitten had enjoyed being petted, and now all that work was for nothing!

It wasn't Ginger's fault, but Rosie knew that Ginger was never going to let one of the builders pick her up. She'd run away from the girls from the rescue shelter, and that was before Ginger had had a week of scary builders invading her home.

Ginger would let Rosie feed her, and pet her. But Rosie was on one side of the fence, and Ginger was on the other. How was Rosie ever going to get the kitten out?

Chapter Eight

"Oh, Rosie, she was so close!" Grandma came hurrying over. "That was such bad luck. She really seemed to be trusting you." Grandma shook her head. "I just can't believe how patient you've been with her. You deserve to have her, Rosie, you really do."

Rosie gave her a grateful hug.

"Well, what are we going to do now?" Grandma wondered. "How on earth are we going to get Ginger out? She's too frightened to let anyone pick her up – you might just about be able to do it, but those builders can't let you go on to the site, even if they want to. If you hurt yourself, they could be in real trouble. I suppose we're just going to have to call the rescue shelter and get them to do it."

Rosie nodded. "I hadn't thought of the rescue shelter people coming back. They'd probably have to use a net or a cage, wouldn't they?" Rosie shuddered. "It's better than staying where she is. It's really dangerous here. But Ginger will be scared and run away again.... Oh, Grandma, there's got to be a better way!" Rosie sat down on the grass, thinking hard. "Well, I can't go in, so Ginger has to come out, doesn't she? But I just don't see how – this fence is like a prison, even for a cat."

Grandma sighed. "I have a feeling we're going to be here for a while." She patted Rosie on the shoulder. "You stay here and watch for her. I'll head home and make us some sandwiches. I won't be long." Rosie looked up suddenly. "Don't worry. I'll bring more ham for Ginger, too. But if we do catch that kitten, she'll need to learn to like something other than ham…."

Rosie watched her walk slowly down the road. She was so lucky having Grandma. If Grandma didn't have her after school, she'd never even have met Ginger. But mostly because Grandma was never in a rush. Grandma didn't mind spending an hour sitting outside a building site, watching for a kitten. That was pretty special.

Rosie turned back to the fence and stared at it hopelessly. If only she could climb over it! The builders were starting to leave now. Once they were gone, no one would see.... But Grandma would be really upset with her. She'd trusted Rosie to be sensible, leaving her here. Rosie couldn't let her down.

Rosie shook the fence, making it rattle. It was even taller than the one at school around the playing field. Then she stopped, and stared at the fence thoughtfully. The one at school had holes in, where people had leaned on it over the years, and one place where some of the older boys had decided to dig a tunnel underneath when they were bored.

Rosie couldn't get *over* the fence, but maybe she could get *under* it. Or at least the kitten could....

She crouched down and peered at the base of the fence. It ran along the ground, and it was held tightly between posts, so there were no gaps – yet. Rosie started to hunt for a likely place. Oh! Yes, here.... Something had already done half the job for her. Maybe that fox they'd seen before. Whatever it was had dug a hole a few inches deep under the fence before it gave up.

Rosie lifted the fence carefully. She was pretty sure that Ginger could fit under there, but she'd better dig it out a bit more, just to be certain. Rosie found a big stone and started to scrape the earth away as fast as she could, looking up every so often to check for Ginger.

The farm was quiet. Ginger's ears and whiskers stopped their panicky twitching at last. She poked her nose out from under the large black tarp where she'd dashed after that loud bang. No noise of diggers, no rumbling wheels, no men shouting. It should be safe now. Ginger slid out, still listening carefully. There was an odd scritch-scratching noise coming from across the yard. Was it that fox who'd been stealing from the garbage? She'd seen it again the other night.

There was no smell now, so it couldn't be a fox. Ginger padded slowly out into the yard, following the noise. It sounded like something was digging under the fence. Maybe it *was* that fox. The fur rose up on Ginger's back. She crept around the back of the tractor, and threw a quick look over at the fence.

It was her! The girl! She was still there! The noise hadn't scared her away. And she was digging under the fence. Was she trying to come in?

Ginger gave a hopeful meow, and crept across the yard toward Rosie, glancing around, just in case.

Rosie dropped the stone. "Ginger!" Rosie sat up on her heels eagerly, grabbing the fence to look through the wire, and Ginger paused, scared by the sudden movement. "Oh, I'm sorry...." Rosie rocked back on her knees, leaving a space between herself and the fence. "I didn't mean to scare you, Ginger. I'm just so glad to see you!" Rosie dug the last tiny handful of fishy cat treats out of the packet that she'd been keeping in her bag, and scattered them for Ginger – on Rosie's side of the fence.

"Come on, Ginger … please...."

The tiny kitten sniffed thoughtfully. The smell was familiar. Those strange round things she'd found before! They were from the girl, too? Ginger preferred ham, but she wouldn't complain. Still, she had to get under the fence to get them.

Ginger padded closer, peering through the hole. It seemed big enough. She'd been hoping to find the girl, and a way out. Now the girl had made her one. Ginger stared up at Rosie, her big green eyes hopeful, and almost trusting. She would do it.

Rosie stared back, her eyes hopeful, too, desperate for Ginger to trust her. "Hey, little one," Rosie whispered. "Come on…."

Ginger crouched down, and started to wriggle under the fence, the wire just skimming the fur on her back. She popped out the other side, shook herself, and then sneezed from the dust. Then she eyed the cat treats eagerly.

"Go on, they're for you!" Rosie reassured her, and Ginger gobbled them down, a curious expression on her face. Such an odd flavor. But she could get used to it. Ginger licked her whiskers and looked up at Rosie. Then she put one tiny paw on her knee, and meowed.

More?

"Are you still hungry?" Rosie smiled. "You could come back to Grandma's with me. She's making ham sandwiches, your favorite." Rosie stood up slowly, and stepped backward. "You coming? Hmmm? Coming, Ginger?"

And Ginger padded after Rosie, her tail waving, following her home.

Out Now:

Sophie often sees her elderly neighbor, Mr. Jenkins, walking his Labrador puppy, Buttons. Sophie loves the little dog and wishes she had one, too.

Buttons is sweet, but she's so active that she is becoming too much for Mr. Jenkins to handle. Then one day, Mr. Jenkins is injured at home, and Buttons knows she needs to find Sophie to help. Buttons gets out of the yard and takes off down the road, searching for Sophie. Will she find Sophie in time to help Mr. Jenkins?

Pet Rescue Adventures

Max the Missing Puppy

HOLLY WEBB

Molly is thrilled when her family adopts a beautiful Old English sheepdog puppy. She names the puppy Max, and soon, the two are inseparable.

Max misses Molly when she's at school, and he longs for her to come home and play. One day, Max gets out of the house through an open window and sets off to find Molly. But the world is a scary place for a puppy, and before long, Max is lost and in danger. How will he ever find Molly and get back home safely?

Pet Rescue Adventures

The Frightened Kitten

HOLLY WEBB

Maddie loves her beautiful new tortoiseshell kitten, Cookie. She spends all her time with the kitten and can't wait until Cookie is old enough to go out in the yard.

Before long, Cookie is able to venture outside. She loves being in the yard, but there are two neighborhood cats that are always trying to chase her away. Soon, Cookie is too scared to go out and spends most of her time hiding under Maddie's bed. Can Maddie find a way to help Cookie feel brave enough to play outside again?

HOLLY WEBB

Holly Webb started out as a children's book editor, and wrote her first series for the publisher she worked for. She has been writing ever since, with more than 90 books to her name. Holly lives in England with her husband and three young sons. She has three pet cats, who are always nosing around when Holly is trying to type on her laptop.

For more information
about Holly Webb visit:

www.holly-webb.com
www.tigertalesbooks.com